DATE DUE

WEIRD
RACES

By K.C. Kelley

The Child's World

Published by The Child's World®
1980 Lookout Drive
Mankato, MN 56003-1705
800-599-READ
www.childsworld.com

The Child's World®: Mary Berendes, Publishing Director
The Design Lab: Design and production

Photo credits
Cover: Johnson Creek Fire & EMS, Wisconsin/Lloyd Schultz
(top); AP/Wide World (left); Mike King (right)

Interior: AP/Wide World: 6, 17, 22; Corbis: 9; dreamstime.
com: 14; Getty Images: 18; iStock: 5, 21; Johnson Creek Fire &
EMS, Wisconsin/Lloyd Schultz: 10; Mike King: 13 (2).

Library of Congress Cataloging-in-Publication Data
Kelley, K. C.
 Weird races / by K. C. Kelley.
     p. cm.
 Includes bibliographical references and index.
 ISBN 978-1-60954-376-1 (library bound: alk. paper)
 1. Racing—Juvenile literature. I. Title.
 GV1018.K45 2011
 796—dc22   2010042898

Printed in the United States of America
Mankato, Minnesota
December, 2010
PA02070

*Above: Ostrich racing is
popular both in Africa
and in Arizona at the
annual Chandler Ostrich
Festival. See page 22 to
find out more!*

*For more information
about the bed race on
page 1, turn to page 10.*

TABLE OF CONTENTS

Right: Twenty-five crazy people ran a marathon at the North Pole in 2010. See page 12 for more details.

Racing into Weirdness!

The very first race was probably between an early human and a large animal with **fangs**. The animal probably won. Soon after, people were racing against each other. They've been racing ever since! Racing is more than just feet vs. feet, however. You've heard of auto racing and horse racing ... even boat racing. But that's not all that people race. Here's a look at some of the wildest, wackiest, weirdest races in the world!

On your mark . . . get set . . . go! First one to the finish line gets to read this book!

FAST FACT!

Look for "Fast Facts" (get it?!) like these about the races inside! And if you're racing a tiger, you have to run 25 mph (40 kph) to get away.

FAST FACT!

The U.S. Lawnmower Racing Association (USLRA) has been holding races since 1962. They put on more than a dozen races each year!

Where's the Grass?

Have you seen someone using a ride-on lawnmower? Maybe the gardener at your school uses one. The rider drives the mower slowly and easily over the grass. The mower cuts the grass. But what if you could get that mower really moving fast? That's what lawnmower racing is. Drivers compete on dirt courses (that's right . . . no grass) in **souped-up** ride-on mowers. It's all about speed, not about having a nice lawn!

This lawnmower racer doesn't have to worry about raking up after he's finished!

A Barrel of Fun

The old song "Roll Out the Barrel" has a different meaning in Italy. A famous barrel race has been held in the small town of Montepulciano (mon-tay-pool-CHA-noh) since 1373. That's more than 600 years of barrels! The racers are called *springitori* (spring-ih-TOR-ee). They work in pairs to push heavy barrels through the racecourse. The trick is that much of the course is uphill, which makes pushing much harder! Each pair races through one of the town's neighborhoods. The winners get a special silk banner called a *palio* (PAHL-yo). They also get sore arms!

Racers wear sturdy gloves and colorful jerseys while rolling the large, wooden barrels . . . uphill!

Another famous Italian race is held twice a year in Siena. The *Il Palio* is a horse race around the town square. Ten riders take part. More than 60,000 people crowd the square to watch the wild 90-second race!

FAST FACT!

Bed-racing tip from the pros: Put your smallest, lightest team member on the bed. Less weight means a faster push!

Let's hope these firefighting bed racers are not on the way to a real fire! Many places use bed races to raise money for charity.

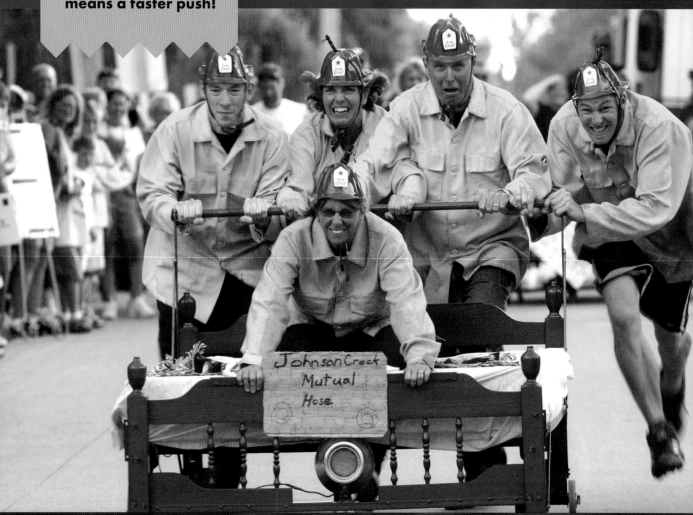

Fast Asleep . . . Really Fast!

You probably think of your bed as a place to rest. That's not the case with these beds—they can really *move*! In bed races, a five-member team pushes a rolling bed down a course. The track often includes pushing the bed up or down a hill. Four people push. The fifth person just stays on the bed. Look for teams of people wearing strange costumes at a bed race near you!

Running Cold

A **marathon** is one of the hardest races that people run. Athletes run more than 26 miles (42 km)! The best runners take less than three hours to finish. The craziest marathoners, however, race at the North Pole. That's right. In a place where it only gets above 0° F (-18 C) about six days a year, people take a nice, easy, 26-mile jog over snow and ice and through biting wind. Why? The answer would only make sense to a crazed runner.

To battle the cold and wind on the course, runners dress in protective gear (inset).

FAST FACT!

Twenty-five people ran the 2010 North Pole Marathon. The temperature reached −4° F (−20 C). Joep Rozendal of the Netherlands finished in just over five hours to win the men's race. Emer Dooley of Ireland won the women's race in five hours, 56 minutes.

2009 North Pole Marathon

2

www.np

In 2009, Switzerland's Yvon Labarthe was the World Cup Series champ in Street Luge.

The helmet and heavy leather clothing help protect riders during high-speed tumbles.

Lying Down on the Job

Normally, a **luge** (LOOZSH) is a special sled made for zooming down frozen hills. Luges slide on a carefully-made ice track surrounded by high walls. A few years ago, some skateboard lovers saw the luge and thought, hey, why don't we do that on the street? After a few experiments, street luge was born. Riders wearing heavy leather clothes and helmets lie on long, wheeled sleds. Then they zip feet-first down twisting, turning, downhill courses. Top riders can reach amazing speeds of 60–70 mph (97–113 kph).

Hold On Tight, Honey!

In Finland, a strange sport called wife-carrying was created more than a hundred years ago. The race is just what it says: A man races over a course while carrying his wife. To make it harder, the track has water jumps, barriers, and swings. A few years ago, a wife-carrier from Estonia figured out that the best way to carry his wife was upside-down . . . on his back! It looked odd, but Estonians have won 11 straight World Wife-Carrying Championships.

This wife-carrying method works, but it must be pretty uncomfortable for the passenger!

FAST FACT!

What happens if you drop your wife? Well, you get a 15-second penalty.

FAST FACT!

Why Gloucestershire? That's the longtime home of famous cheesemakers.

Who will reach the bottom first—the running, bouncing people or the rolling cheese?

Cheesy Does It!

Which do you think is faster: a **wheel** of cheese or a person? For over 200 years, people in Gloucestershire (GLOSS-tur-shur), England have tried to find out. Racers start at the top of a steep hill. A cheese wheel is rolled down and people follow—quickly. The idea is simple: Catch the cheese. Since the cheese is rolling and people are mostly falling, the cheese is rarely caught. Not surprisingly, this race worries some people. Cheese-chasers are often injured while falling. But the cheese chasing goes on!

Giddyup, Fido!

Do you like to ski? Do you have a dog? Then **skijoring** (SKEE-jor-ing) is for you! Popular in Finland and Sweden, skijoring is when a dog or couple of dogs pull a skier. There are races over courses short and long. All types of dogs can skijor, from huskies to shepherds to Labs. Some skijorers choose to be pulled by horses.

The skijorer has a harness around her waist that is attached to the dog.

FAST FACT!

In some ostrich races, the rider sits right on the bird. In others, the bird pulls a small cart on wheels.

Ostrich riders hold on tight as their birds charge toward the finish line.

Who Needs a Horse?

Horse racing is certainly not weird. But what about racing other animals? In Africa, people have raced ostriches for many years. Folks in Arizona hold the annual Chandler Ostrich Festival, which includes racing. Then there's camel racing, popular in the Middle East and Australia. The annual Camel Cup in Alice Springs, Australia, attracts a dozen riders and hundreds of fans. Another animal you might see race doesn't need a rider. Look for pig racing at a county fair near you.

Glossary

fangs—sharp, pointed teeth

luge—a sled on which the rider lies with feet facing downhill

marathon—a running race that covers 26 miles, 385 yards (42.2 km)

skijoring—a sport in which skiers are pulled by dogs or horses

souped-up—built to have added power or speed

wheel—in this case, this means a large cheese in the shape of a hockey puck.

Web Sites

For links to learn more about weird sports: **childsworld.com/links**

Note to Parents, Teachers, and Librarians: We routinely verify our Web links to make sure they are safe and active sites. So encourage your readers to check them out!

Index